To Lahn and Livia with love from Bubba

This edition published 2011 by
Kane Miller, A Division of EDC Publishing

For information contact:
Kane Miller, A Division of EDC Publishing
P.O. Box 470663
Tulsa, OK 74147-0663
www.kanemiller.com
www.edcpub.com

Library of Congress Control Number: 2010939043

Manufactured by Regent Publishing Services, Hong Kong
Printed April 2011 in ShenZhen, Guangdong, China

1 2 3 4 5 6 7 8 9 10

ISBN: 978-1-61067-017-3

Many thanks to Maria Weisbin for the inspired writing of this edition.

Acorns
and Stew,
Too

Ruth Orbach

Kane Miller
A DIVISION OF EDC PUBLISHING

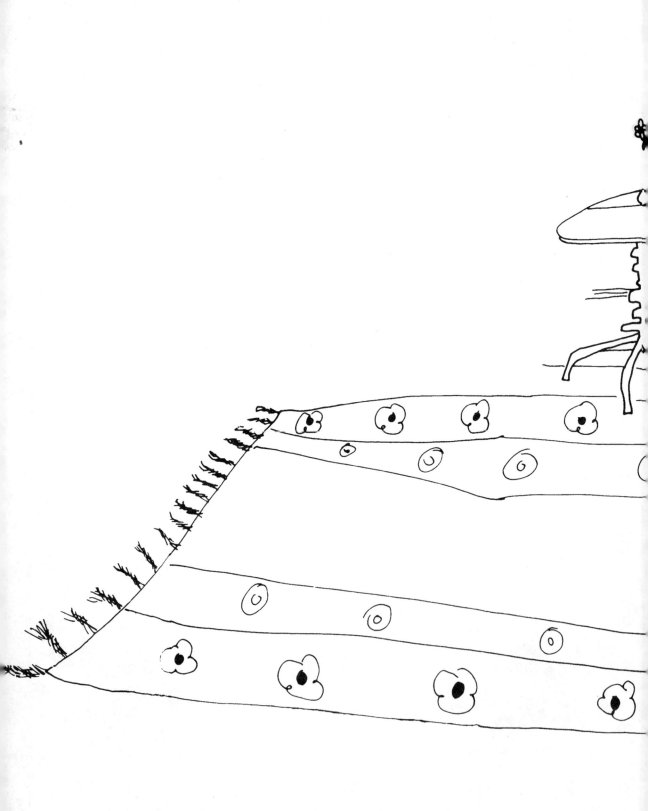

Lenore had a problem.

She loved her house
with its yellow door.
She liked her street
with its birds and trees.

Her room was cozy.

She adored her everyday breakfast of pancakes, butter and jam.

And of course, there was Sam.

But most of all, Lenore loved the ducks that lived by the lake. Every day she visited the park with a bag of bread just for them.

Once she brought them leftover fish. And once she even brought them porridge. They didn't quite know what to make of that.

Lenore loved the ducks, and the ducks
loved Lenore.

This was Lenore's problem: Winter
was coming, and the ducks had
to fly away. And she would miss
them terribly.

Leaves fell from the trees. (The ducks tried to stick them back on.)

Icy rain fell from the sky. The ducks were cold
and hungry and tired.

"Don't go yet," Lenore begged the ducks. "There must be something a girl can do. I'll think, and I'll find a way."

Lenore thought and thought,
and she found a way.

She measured and marked and hammered
and sawed, while Sam kept her company.
"Thanks, Sam," she said.
"Meow," he said.

Then she painted with brushes and big pails
of paint. (She put down newspaper first.)

Lenore brought the ducks a big pot of stew.
And she dug a hole and filled it with acorns.

"Don't fly away," she told them. "Friends stay
friends even in winter."

The next day, Lenore rose early.
She smiled as she cut and stitched
and snipped and sewed the old
blankets and sweaters and thin,
worn rugs she'd gathered.

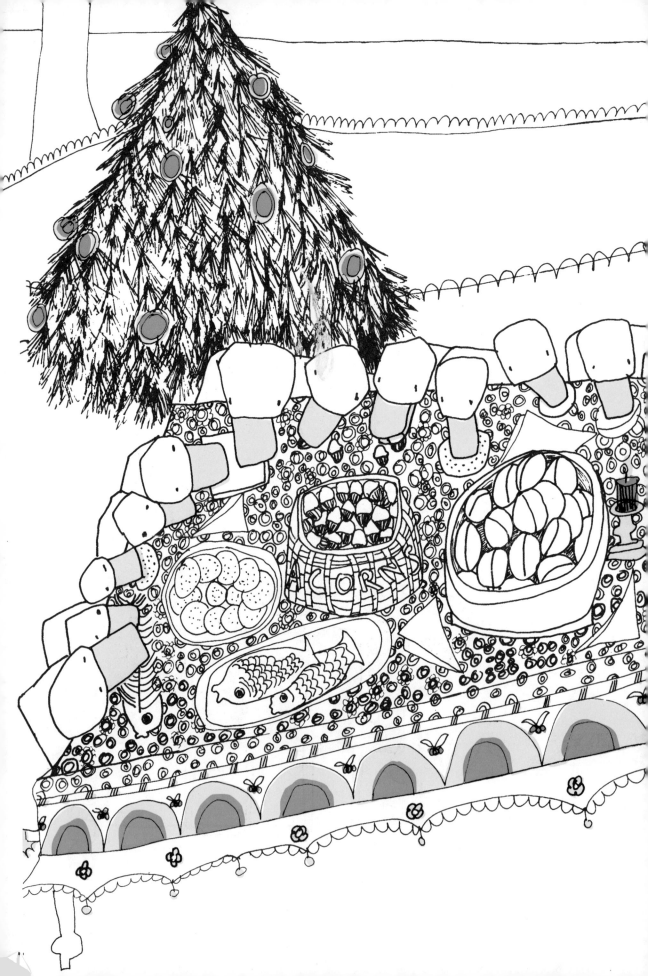

When the ducks awoke on the first day of winter down by the lake … Look! They found a feast: fish and rolls, porridge and biscuits, cake and plums, acorns and stew.

Everything a duck could want.

After they'd eaten their fill and stored the rest in pots and pans, they lined up, and Lenore buttoned them into their new winter coats. They did not fly away. They stayed.

So, if you go down to the
lake in winter and see
a duck in an overcoat,
you'll know it's a friend of
Lenore's ... and yours.

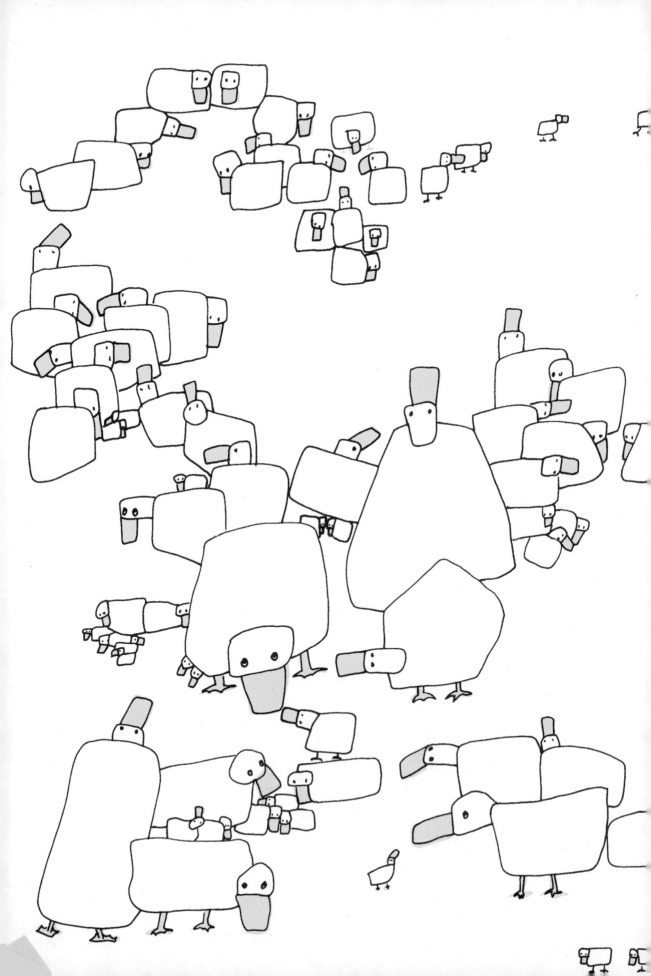